The Hide-and-Scare BEAR

To all at Brisley Primary School,
for showing everyone the kind way to play
and much, much more

First U.S. edition 2016

Library of Congress Catalog Card Number 2015934263

ISBN 978-0-7636-8181-4

15 16 17 18 19 20 TLF 10 9 8 7 6 5 4 3 2 1

Printed in Dongguan, Guangdong, China

This book was typeset in Diotima.
The illustrations were done in mixed media.

TEMPLAR BOOKS
an imprint of
Candlewick Press
99 Dover Street
Somerville, Massachusetts 02144
www.candlewick.com

The Hide-and-Scare
BEAR

by Ivan Bates

templar books
an imprint of Candlewick Press

There once
lived a bear who
was not very good.
He didn't think about
others or behave
as he should.

He picked his nose.

He gobbled his food.

Not a "please"
or a "thank-you"—
he was horribly rude!

But the worst
thing was that
this mischievous bear
liked playing a game
he called Hide and Scare.

He would
creep up on
others and
count up to
three . . .

then jump out with a

ROAR!

from behind
a tall tree.

"Hide and Scare,"
growled the bear,
"is such marvelous fun!"
And he laughed and he laughed
as he watched them all run.

The animals
gathered. Enough
was enough!
Owl said to the crowd,
"We need to get tough!"

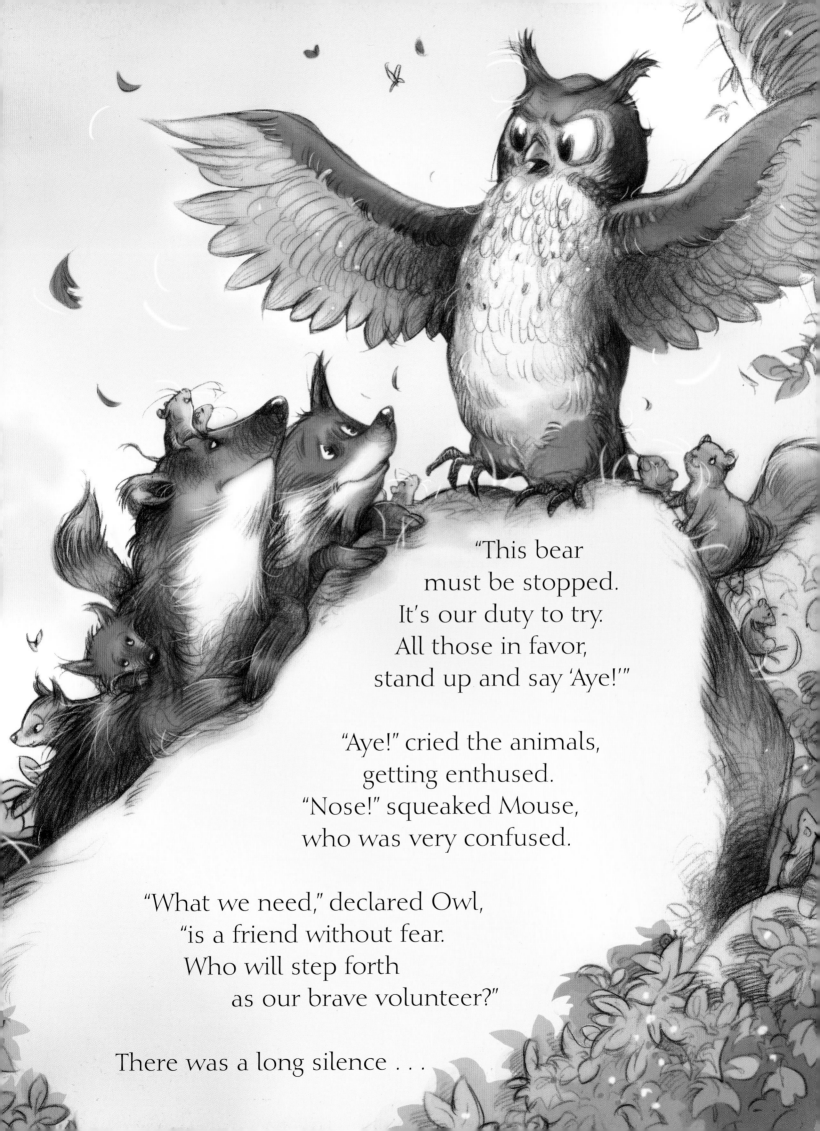

"This bear
must be stopped.
It's our duty to try.
All those in favor,
stand up and say 'Aye!'"

"Aye!" cried the animals,
getting enthused.
"Nose!" squeaked Mouse,
who was very confused.

"What we need," declared Owl,
"is a friend without fear.
Who will step forth
as our brave volunteer?"

There was a long silence . . .

then a quiet voice said,
"I can help. Not with anger,
but with kindness instead."

Standing alone,
with a twitchy pink nose
stood a soft little rabbit
who then said, "I propose . . .

that maybe this bear's
not as bad as you say.
He's just never been shown
the kind way to play.
What he needs, I believe,
is some gentle advice—
a short rabbit lesson
on how to be nice."

"Nonsense!"
scoffed Badger.

"You're crazy!"
Squirrel squeaked.

"Preposterous!"
Fox laughed.

ROAR!

Out Bear leaped.

The animals ran
as fast as they could,
except for brave Rabbit;
there she still stood!

The Hide-and-Scare Bear
hadn't seen this before,
so he snarled and he growled
and he roared even more!

But Rabbit just sat there.
Bear stamped
and he growled,

and he howled very deeply
and snarled very loud.

Then, sad and exhausted,
Bear finally stopped.
   With a sigh
    and a whimper
     he slumped
       on a rock.

"If you're finished,"
said Rabbit,
"I have some advice.
It might suit you better
to start acting nice.

Try showing kindness to
those that you meet.
No more snarling and growling
and stamping your feet.

You could try shaking paws.
You could wave and say hi.
Give a smile or a bow when a
friend passes by."

"But for those who are special,
just one thing is right.
Hold open your arms and . . .

HUG THEM TIGHT!"

"Thank you," said Bear.

"You've helped me to see
how wonderful kindness
and cuddles can be.
From this moment on,
I'll be changing my ways.
I'll be giving out hugs
for the rest of my days!"

And do you know what?
That bear changed for good.
He used manners and kindness
every way that he could.
Now no one was worried
about Hide and Scare.
Instead they got hugs
when they met up with Bear.

Finally
everyone was
getting along . . .

though a hug from a bear can
be rather strong!